SAM WU
is <u>NOT</u> afraid of
ZOMBIES

EGMONT

EGMONT
We bring stories to life

First published in Great Britain in 2020
by Egmont UK Limited
2 Minster Court, 10th Floor, London EC3R 7BB

Text copyright © 2020 Katie Tsang and Kevin Tsang
Illustration copyright © 2020 Nathan Reed
Additional interior illustrations copyright © 2020 Egmont Ltd

ISBN 978 1 4052 9572 7

www.egmont.co.uk

A CIP catalogue record for this title is available from the British Library

70717/001

MIX
Paper from
responsible sources
FSC® C020471

FOR OUR DAUGHTER, EVIE

-Katie & Kevin Tsang

CONTENTS

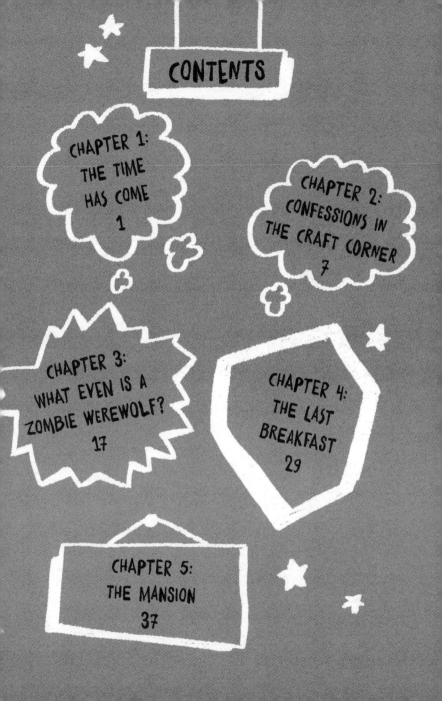

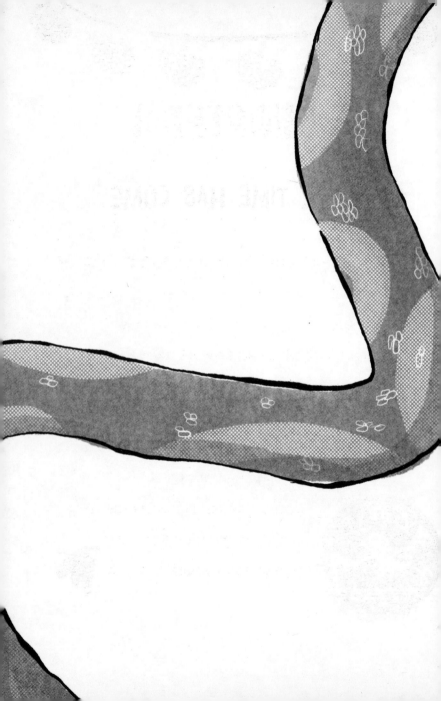

CHAPTER 1

THE TIME HAS COME

My name is **Sam Wu** and I am <u>NOT</u> afraid of zombies. Not zombie werewolves, not mummy zombies, or any other kind of zombies.

I'll admit that I had to work my way up to not being afraid of zombies. I don't actually know if there is anything scarier than an undead zombie chasing you and your friends.

But I'm getting ahead of myself.

Before I faced the zombies, I'd already come face to face with ghosts, sharks, the dark, and spiders. And I'd proven again and again, how **NOT** afraid I was.

Little did I know this was all to prepare me for my greatest challenge yet.

Because not only are zombies the **SCARIEST** thing I've ever faced (not that I'm afraid of them) but on top of everything, I had to work together with my greatest nemesis.

Ralph Philip Zinkerman the Third.

Ralph was the reason I had to prove I was brave in the first place. He was the one who started calling me Scaredy Cat Sam when the incident that will *never be spoken of again*[1] happened at

---

[1] All you need to know about that is it involved an Astro Blast simulator, the Ghost King, and me being very brave despite a pair of slightly wet pants.

the Space Museum.

But then after the *incident*, Ralph and I had
to work together to face the dark, and Ralph
even became a part of my very
own **SPACE BLASTERS**
crew[2]. But that didn't
make us best buddies
or anything like that.
It's a little confusing
when your nemesis
suddenly becomes part of
your team. Or when they suddenly need your

---

[2] **SPACE BLASTERS** is the greatest show in the entire universe! It's about
Spaceman Jack and **Captain Jane** and all the adventures they have on their
spaceship TUBS, which stands for The Universe's Best Spaceship.
Whenever I get a little nervous, I just imagine what they would do.

help with something. But as **Captain Jane** from SPACE BLASTERS always says, you never know who might turn out to be an ally in a time of need.

I think that is also what my dad means when he says it's important to 'be the bigger person'. He doesn't actually mean be **BIGGER**, which is what I thought when he first told me that.

So when Ralph and his twin sister **Regina** (who is about a million times nicer than him) asked me and my best friends **Zoe** and **Bernard** to help them,

I knew I had no choice.

I had to do what **Captain Jane** and **Spaceman Jack** (and my dad) would want me to do.

It was finally time to face…

THE ZOMBIE WEREWOLF!

CHAPTER 2

CONFESSIONS IN THE CRAFT CORNER

It all started when I noticed that Ralph and Regina kept falling asleep in class.

Ralph might be my nemesis, but I didn't want Regina to get in trouble, so I threw a balled-up piece of paper at her head to wake her up. It just bounced off her, and she kept sleeping.

"Regina!" I whispered as loud as I dared. Nothing. Ralph drooled a little bit next to her.

"Regina!" I tried again. No response.

When our teacher Ms Winkleworth turned back to the board, I threw an eraser at Regina.

Unfortunately, I don't have great aim. The eraser hit Ralph instead.

"Ow!" he said, jolting awake and rubbing the back of his head. Regina must have heard him, because she woke up too, blinking sleepily. Ralph looked around and saw me staring straight at him. Then he threw the eraser back, *way* harder than I had.

"Ow!" I said, as the eraser hit me in the nose.

"What is going on?" said Ms Winkleworth, who had turned around just in time to see the eraser bounce off my nose. "Ralph, are you throwing things?"

"Sam Wu threw his eraser at me first!" said Ralph.

Sam, is that true?" said Ms Winkleworth.

I wanted to explain that it was because Ralph and Regina had been sleeping and I was trying to help, but I didn't want to be a tattler (even though Ralph had just told on me). So I tried to be the bigger person and just shrugged. "It was an accident," I said. "It just . . . flew out of my hands. Like magic."

"Maybe it was a ghost!" said Bernard, who always has my back. He is one of my best friends and is the smartest person I know. He's basically a walking dictionary.

"*Exactly*," I said, giving Ms Winkleworth my most serious face.

Ms Winkleworth sighed. "Sam, erasers don't just fly out of people's hands," she said. Then she went and wrote both of our names on the board and circled them. "You two will both have to stay inside today at break and help tidy the craft corner."

"That's not fair," Ralph whined. "Sam Wu started it."

"Well, next time you should both think twice about throwing erasers in class," said Ms Winkleworth.

༄

And that was how I found myself in the craft corner with my nemesis, Ralph Zinkerman the Third.

"You should do the tidying," he said when Ms Winkleworth was at her desk going through some papers. "This is your fault!"

"I was trying to help you!" I spluttered.

"Well, I was trying to help Regina, but you were asleep too! I could have told on you, you know.

But I didn't." I held my head a little higher when I said this.

I was not asleep!

Ralph said.

You were! And you drooled.

"I do **NOT** drool," Ralph said with a snort. He is the master of snorts.

"You did," I said. Then I frowned. "Why are you both so tired?"

Ralph sighed and sat down. "None of your business," he said as he held back a yawn. "And I'm not tired."

"I'm just trying to help," I said.

"Why?" said Ralph suspiciously.

I had to think about that one. It was true, Ralph was my nemesis. He *always* made fun of me in front of everyone and he called me names like Scaredy Cat Sam and Sam Wu-ser (which he thinks is funny because he makes my last name sound like loser).

But even if Ralph wasn't always my friend, Regina was. And I had a feeling that whatever was bothering Ralph would be bothering her too. Plus, I'd learned from **SPACE BLASTERS** that sometimes being a good Captain is checking in on all of your crew, even the ones you don't like as much.

"Because we're in the same crew," I said.

Ralph snorted (like I said, he is the master

of snorts) and rolled his eyes. "That was one camping trip in the woods," he said. "And don't think it means we're best friends or anything now. Because we're not."

"Suit yourself," I said, and turned to organize some paint brushes. I tried to whistle too, to show how much I wasn't bothered, but I don't know how to whistle, so instead I kind of just blew air out of my mouth and hooted a bit.

"Why are you making train noises?" Ralph said. "You are so weird."

"I'm just whistling," I said. "Minding my own business."

Ralph scowled. "Fine! I'll tell you. Regina will probably tell you anyway. She's convinced that you and your friends are the only ones who can help us. I don't know why."

"Really?" I said, standing up a little straighter. It was nice to feel appreciated.

Ralph paused and then looked around to make sure nobody could hear him. "Do you remember what Regina said is trapped in our basement?"

I gulped. Ralph couldn't be talking about what I thought he was talking about . . . could he?

"You don't mean . . . " I couldn't even say it.

Ralph nodded solemnly.

"It's louder than ever. We can't sleep at night because we're worried it's going to get out."

I gulped again.

"And eat us," he added, in case it wasn't clear. "We don't know what to do."

"Well," I said, trying to show how brave I was even though I was starting to sweat, "the first thing we need to do is to get everyone in our crew back together if we're going to face . . . **THE ZOMBIE WEREWOLF**."

CHAPTER 3

WHAT EVEN IS A ZOMBIE WEREWOLF?

My best friends Zoe and Bernard couldn't believe it when I told them we needed to have a top-secret meeting with Ralph and Regina that day at lunch.

"What?" said Zoe. "But Ralph just got you in trouble!"

"Trust me," I said. "It's serious. They need our help."

"With what?" asked Bernard. "Being their personal alarm clocks?"

"Yeah, why do they keep falling asleep in class?" said Zoe.

"They need help with the *zombie werewolf*," I said, waggling my eyebrows to make sure Zoe and Bernard knew exactly how serious this was.

"Ohh!" said Zoe, and Bernard's mouth dropped a little bit open.

They definitely knew what I meant. Regina had been telling us for a while about this mysterious zombie werewolf in their basement, and each time she did, I said that of course we'd come to help her. But I never thought we actually would have to. **Captain Jane** on **SPACE BLASTERS** says that you should never offer something if you can't follow

through, and I guess I'm learning that the
hard way.

"Sam, we don't know anything about zombie
werewolves!" Zoe said, looking nervous. "That
is too serious and too dangerous for us."

"We're official Ghost Hunters! And Spider Catchers! And snake wranglers! If anyone can do it, we can," I said, with more confidence than I felt. Another thing I've learned on **SPACE BLASTERS** is that sometimes, even if you are scared, you just have to act like you aren't, and sometimes you can trick yourself into being Not Scared. This doesn't always work for me, but I like to try it anyway.

"What *do* any of those things have to do with zombie werewolves?" Zoe went on.

I paused.

"Nothing!" Zoe said, throwing her arms in the air.

20

She was right.

"Well, you might have a point," I said slowly. "We don't know anything about zombie werewolves. But we didn't know anything about sharks or ghosts either, until we did some research." I turned to Bernard with a big grin. "Are you thinking what I'm thinking, Bernard?"

Bernard loves research so I thought that this would *definitely* get him on board.

But he just scratched his head. "I don't know, Sam. Some things, even research can't prepare you for. I'm not even sure what a zombie werewolf *is*. Are you?"

"And what if it's a trap?" said Zoe. "What if Ralph is inviting us over just to use us as **BAIT** for the zombie werewolf? That sounds like something he would do."

This was **<u>NOT</u>** going well.

"Regina wouldn't do that," I said, but I wished Zoe hadn't put that idea in my head. "And Ralph can be evil, but he isn't *that* evil." At least I hoped he wasn't.

Just then, Regina bounded over to us, with a huge smile on her face. Ralph was trailing behind her, sulking.

"Ralph told me the good news!" she said breathlessly. "You're going to help us with our zombie werewolf problem!"

"You bet we are!" I said.

Zoe and Bernard groaned.

"I knew we could count on you," said Regina.

A very small part of me regretted previously telling Regina so confidently that we could help with the zombie werewolf. I hadn't thought we'd actually have to face it. It is like that one time on **SPACE BLASTERS** when **Spaceman Jack** offered to help save a whole planet from invading evil aliens, and then when the aliens arrived he realized just how scary they were, but he stayed to help because he'd said he would. Plus my dad always says that . . .

"A WU IS ONLY AS GOOD AS THEIR WORD."

But still, I wondered why *now* was the time we had to take action. It wouldn't be the worst thing in the world to wait a little bit before facing the zombie werewolf.

"So have things got worse?" I asked, trying to keep my voice casual.[3]

Regina lowered her voice. "We are in *desperate* need of help, and soon. I think we're running out of time. The zombie werewolf is getting stronger. At least it's definitely getting louder. It could break out of our basement at **ANY MOMENT!**"

"Erm, have you thought about telling your parents?" said Bernard. "That sounds like something they might want to know about."

[3] It is very difficult to sound casual when you are talking about something as scary as a zombie werewolf.

Regina waved her hand in the air like she was flicking a fly out of the way. "We've tried. But they never believe us."

"All they *do* is say that we shouldn't *go* in the basement because it is *off-limits*," added Ralph darkly.

"Probably because there is a zombie werewolf down there," said Bernard. "That makes sense to make it off limits." Then he furrowed his brow and I knew he was thinking extra hard. "How far away is your basement from the rest of the house? Are there windows? Stairs? How many exits are there?"

"See! These are the kinds of things we need to think about," said Regina enthusiastically. "You should all come over this weekend so you can see for yourselves what we're dealing with."

"If we make it to the weekend," Ralph muttered. Then he looked straight at me. "And if you're not too scared to come over, Sam Wu."

"I'm **NOT** too scared," I said, even though my heart was beating very fast. "Of course we're coming over. We're going to come over and we're going to solve the mystery of the zombie werewolf. Once and for all." I gave Ralph a triumphant look.

He looked back at me sceptically, and I expected a signature Ralph snort, but at least he didn't do that.

Zoe sighed loudly. "Well, I guess that's settled then. Your parents can call our parents?"

Regina and Ralph nodded.

"I still don't think you'll be able to do anything useful," said Ralph, "but Regina is convinced."

"Ralph, you know we don't have any other options," said Regina. "They're our only hope!"

Ralph snorted this time but didn't say anything else.

And I tried **NOT** to panic.

CHAPTER 4

THE LAST BREAKFAST

My parents were thrilled that I was going over to Ralph's house.

"I told you that things would work out, Sam," said my dad at breakfast on Saturday. "I knew that you and Ralph would become friends eventually. I'm proud of you."

I didn't know how to explain to my dad that this was a **MUCH BIGGER SITUATION** than

the history between Ralph and me. So I just
took another bite of my congee[4]
and tried to enjoy it. If things

didn't go well today, it
might just be the last time
I ever ate it.

Now that it was actually
time to face a zombie werewolf, I was starting
to have **SERIOUS** second thoughts about
going over to Ralph and Regina's house.
What was I thinking? I should have listened
to Zoe and Bernard. And now if anything bad
happened, it was all going to be my fault. I
might be leading everyone into certain doom!

My little sister Lucy came twirling into the
kitchen, with her cat Butterbutt right behind
her. I realized I needed a moment alone with

---

[4] Congee is a delicious porridge made of rice. It's my *favourite* thing to
have for breakfast.

Lucy, to ask her to look after my pet snake Fang in case the zombie werewolf got me. Lucy is one of the few people brave enough to handle my ferocious, man-eating snake[5].

YOWWWL!

[5] Technically Fang doesn't have any real fangs, and I've never actually caught him eating anybody, but he's definitely the fiercest snake I've ever seen.

31

Luckily, just then the phone rang. My dad answered and started speaking in Cantonese[6], so I knew it was probably family in Hong Kong which meant he'd be a while.

"Lucy," I said, putting on my most grown-up voice. "I have something important to ask you. But you can't tell anyone, okay?"

"Okay!" said Lucy, with her mouth full of congee. "I love secrets!"

"Lucy, it's serious," I said.

"You think everything is serious," she said, swinging her legs under her chair and kicking me.

"This time it really is!" I said. "Do you want to know or not?"

"Of course I want to know. I like to know **EVERYTHING**." She grinned.

---

[6] Cantonese is a form of Chinese that people speak in Hong Kong, which is where my parents are from. When my mum is really mad at me, she yells at me in Cantonese, so that I know she is being serious.

It was true. Lucy was always getting involved in whatever me and my friends were doing. But this time it was too risky.

"I've got to go on a mission today. And it's a dangerous one. Maybe the most dangerous one I've ever done," I said.

"Can I come? I love missions!" she said, taking another big slurp of her congee.

"Lower your voice!" I said, looking around to make sure nobody had heard her. "And no, it's too dangerous. It could be a matter of life and death." I paused. "Which is why I need you to promise me something." I took a deep breath. I didn't want to scare Lucy, but there was nobody else I could ask. "If something happens to me, will you look after Fang?"

33

"What might happen to you?" said Lucy, looking sceptical.

"Just promise me. It's important."

"Okay, okay," said Lucy. "I'll look after Fang,"

"There's also a box under my bed. It's where I keep my most valuable possessions. You can have those too."

"Cool!" said Lucy, starting to stand up.

"Wait!" I said. "You don't get them now! Only if something happens to me."

"Okay, okay," she said, sitting back down. "I have one of those too, you know. But I call mine my treasure chest."

"My box isn't a toy," I said, frowning. "It's full of VERY valuable items. Like rare SPACE BLASTERS collectibles. And some very good art I've drawn. And some shiny rocks I've found that are probably worth millions. You know, that kind of thing."

Lucy nodded. "You can trust me," she said.

"Thanks, Lucy," I said.

"But Sam?"

I looked up.

"Even though I'm pretty excited about getting this special box, I hope nothing bad happens to you."

"Me too, Lucy. Me too."

CHAPTER 5

THE MANSION

And then it was time.

Me, Zoe, and Bernard were about to face our greatest challenge yet. Since Zoe's mum was already taking Zoe's brother Toby to a football game nearby, she offered to drive everyone to Regina and Ralph's.

The doorbell rang. I opened it to Zoe and Bernard with grim expressions on their faces.

"I don't believe what you've got us into," said Zoe.

"I'm trying to stay positive," offered Bernard.

"That's the spirit!" I said.

"But I'm finding it very difficult," he added.

My dad appeared behind us to wave to Zoe's mum and say thank you for driving. But then he stopped when he saw the three of us.

"Why do you all look so glum? It's a beautiful day! You're going to a friend's house. Nothing to frown about."

I managed a half-hearted smile. And then, just in case it was the last time I ever saw him, I gave him a tight hug.

My dad patted my back, surprised at my seemingly random burst of affection. "See you this evening, Sam. I'm picking all of you up later."

"See you later, Dad," I said.

The three of us sat together in the back of Zoe's mum's car. "Okay," I said quietly, so she wouldn't hear us, "what's the plan?"

"You mean you don't have a plan?" said Zoe. "This is even worse than I thought! Usually you have some sort of plan, even if it's a terrible one."

"Well, this time I don't. I was hoping one of you did." I looked at Bernard hopefully.

Bernard shook his head. "I'm still not sure what a zombie werewolf even is."

"It's obviously a werewolf that has been turned into a zombie," I said.

"So it's an undead werewolf," said Bernard. "Which means **IT CAN'T BE KILLED BECAUSE IT'S ALRADY DEAD**."

"Who said anything about killing it?" I whispered back.

"Well, what else are we going to do?" said Zoe. "Put a leash on it and take it for a walk?"

"I don't know!" I said, feeling more flustered by the moment. "Maybe Ralph and Regina will have a plan."

"If Ralph and Regina had a plan, they wouldn't have asked us for help. And they wouldn't be so sleepy all the time either," said Zoe.

Zoe's mum glanced back at us in the rearview mirror. "Everything okay back there? There's an awful lot of whispering going on."

"Everything is fine, Mum," said Zoe.

"If only that was true," moaned Bernard under his breath.

"All right, if you say so," said Zoe's mum as she slowed down the car. "I think their house is this turn here."

I looked out the window, but all I could see was a huge fence covered in ivy with a massive black gate that was as tall as my house.

"Woah," said Bernard, his mouth wide open. "Do Ralph and Regina live in a fortress?"

"It sure looks like it," said Zoe.

The gate slowly creaked open as we pulled up in front of it.

"How do they know we're here?" I said.

"Maybe this place is haunted," said Bernard, scooting closer to me.

"Or maybe they saw us with that security camera," Zoe said, pointing out of the window.

"Your friends must be *super* rich if they have their own guard gate with a security camera," said Toby from the front seat, sounding impressed.

"Toby, that's not polite," said Zoe's mum. Then we went through the gate. "This *is* a very large estate though."

We all stared. At the end of the long driveway was a **HUGE** mansion. It looked a little bit like a castle.

"Is this their own private forest?" said Toby, looking around at the trees on either side of the driveway.

"I knew Ralph and Regina were rich," said Zoe, "but I didn't know they were THIS rich!"

"I didn't know *anyone* was this rich!" said Bernard.

The driveway was so long it took us a little while to actually get to the front of the mansion. Zoe's mum was also driving incredibly slowly, sometimes stopping, because we kept seeing things outside the window.

"Is that a fountain?" said Zoe.

"Look at that statue! It looks like Ralph if Ralph was an old man!" said Bernard.

"Something just moved out there!" I shouted.

"It's just a deer," said Zoe's mum. But she slowed down even more.

By the time we pulled up in front of the mansion, we were so excited, I'd almost forgotten about the zombie werewolf.

Almost.

Ralph and Regina's house had turrets and towers like a castle and it looked like it was four storeys tall. Maybe more. I didn't know people actually lived in houses like this.

But it didn't look especially welcoming.

It looked like the kind of place in fairy tales where a wicked sorcerer or evil queen lived.

Or a zombie werewolf.

"This place is definitely haunted," said Bernard, staring up at it with wide eyes.

"How many people live here?" said Toby.

"I think just Ralph and Regina and their parents," I said.

"And the werewolf," whispered Zoe.

"You kids had better get going," said Zoe's mum. "I've got to get Toby to his match. Sam's dad is picking you all up after dinner, right?"

"Right," we said.

"Well hop to it," she said, nodding at the huge stone steps that led up to the massive front door. "I'll wait here to make sure you get in all right."

We climbed up the steps. By the time we got to the top, Bernard was breathing heavily. "You'd think if they were so rich they could put in an elevator or something!" he panted.

"You ring the bell," said Zoe, nudging me. "This whole thing was your idea."

"Technically, it was Ralph and Regina's idea,"
I said, but I stepped forward. Before I could
ring the bell, the door swung open.

"Hi!" said Regina, grinning at us. "Come on in!
My mum just made cookies."

CHAPTER 6

DEADLY SERIOUS

Ralph and Regina's house looked like a museum on the inside. There were big thick rugs on the floor, paintings of serious-looking people on the walls, and a huge grandfather clock ticking loudly.

There was even a deer head over the fire place and a suit of armour in the corner!

"Your house is nice," I said to Regina as she led us through the house into the kitchen. It looked like there were at least a hundred rooms!

"It's **HUGE!**" said Zoe.

Regina laughed. "We're used to it, I guess."

"Do you ever play hide-and-seek in here?" I asked.

"We used to," said Regina. Then she lowered her voice. "Until the you-know-what."

We all nodded solemnly. I had almost forgotten that there was a zombie werewolf in the basement.

❦

Ralph was sitting in the kitchen at the head of a long table. His chair had such a tall back it looked like he was sitting in a throne. In front of him was a big plate of cookies.

"I thought we should have some snacks while we strategize," he said.

I hated to admit it, but he was right.

This was always what me and Zoe and Bernard did too.

"And since this is my house, I'll be leading the meeting," Ralph said, looking straight at me.

"It's my house too," said Regina, laughing as she grabbed a cookie. "And we invited them over to help us, remember?" She turned to me with a big smile. "I think we should have the same codenames we used when we were camping!"

"This isn't a game, Regina," said Ralph. "It's serious."

"Camping was serious too," said Bernard.

"Not as serious as this," said Ralph. "This is **DEADLY** serious."

We all got quiet. Ralph was right.

"Well, I think you're right about one thing," said Bernard, climbing into one of the giant chairs. "We should definitely have cookies."

～ ～

While we ate our cookies, we asked Ralph and Regina to tell us everything they already knew about the zombie werewolf. Bernard took notes. This is what we found out:

- It is most active at night, but sometimes makes noises in the day time

- It howls – loudly

- Whatever it is doing in the basement sometimes makes the whole house shake

- It is probably very hungry down there because there is no food in the basement

- It has got much louder recently and Ralph and Regina are almost 100% positive it is getting ready to escape

"Now what?" said Ralph. The cookies were done. We'd asked all the questions we could think of.

I looked at Bernard. "Chief Research Officer Bernard," I said, using the **SPACE BLASTERS** codename we'd given him when we first all worked together as a crew, "what do you think? Do we have enough data to proceed?"

Ralph rolled his eyes. "You sound ridiculous," he said with a snort. "Like an actor in a TV show."

"Ralph!" said Regina, swatting his arm. "I told you. We need their help! And I trust Sam. I mean, Captain Sam," she said, grinning at me.

I grinned back. "Thank you, Admiral Regina." Then I looked at Ralph. "I am taking this very seriously, Commander Ralph. We only use our codenames in the **MOST** serious of situations. Like this one."

"Fine, fine," said Ralph. "What *do* you say... *Chief Research Officer* Bernard?"

Bernard scanned his notes and chewed on the end of his pen. Then he took out his thinking glasses, which aren't real glasses, but he puts them on whenever he needs to think really hard about something.

"I say...we need to do more research. But I don't know where to start."

"I do!" said Regina. "Did I mention we have a library?"

Bernard looked so excited I thought he might fall off his chair.

We followed Ralph and Regina out of the kitchen and up a spiral staircase and down a long hallway. I wanted to stop and look in every room, but I knew we had to stay focused.

"Where are your parents?" asked Zoe, pausing to look at a sculpture of a camel in the hallway. "And can I touch this?"

"Anything in the hallways can be touched," said Regina. "If it's on a wall, or on a desk or a bookshelf, don't touch it."

"Yeah. Because that means it is valuable. Or fragile," said Ralph. "Our dad is at the Central Museum. Our parents spend a lot of time there. They donate art and stuff. And our mum is outside gardening. She loves roses."

"So does my Na-Na!" I said.

"Who is that?" said Regina.

"That's what I call my grandma," I explained.

"Our mum grows prize-winning roses," said Ralph. "Has your Na-Na ever won a prize for her roses?"

I felt suddenly very defensive of Na-Na. "Yeah," I said, even though I wasn't sure. "She's won **LOTS** of prizes for her roses. And one time she wrestled an alligator!"

Ralph looked suspicious.

"It's true!" said Zoe, who always backs me up. I gave her a grateful smile.

"That's so cool!" said Regina. "All our grandma knows how to wrestle are her knitting needles."

We reached the end of the hallway and stopped in front of a massive set of double doors. Ralph pushed them open and Bernard gasped.

There were so many books! The shelves went all the way to the ceiling and they had ladders running along them, just like the local library, but this looked way fancier. There were probably a **MILLION** books in there!

"Whoa!" said Zoe.

"This is **YOUR** library?" said Bernard in awe.

"It was my great-great-grandpa's library

originally, and then each generation adds to it," said Ralph proudly. I didn't blame him for being proud. It was a very impressive library. I thought I had a lot of books in my house, and we only had one big bookshelf!

"Well, I hope someone in your family was interested in zombie werewolves," said Zoe, looking around at all the books. "Otherwise, all of these are useless to us."

"Any ideas for how we should start our research?" I said to Bernard. "You are our Chief Research Officer, after all."

"Right," said Bernard, standing a little taller. "General Zoe and Admiral Regina, you look up Zombies in the encyclopedia and take notes on anything you think might be helpful. Captain Sam and Commander Ralph, you do the same with werewolves." He pointed at a computer in the corner. "And I'll go online and see if there have been any reports of zombie werewolves before."

I didn't really want to partner with Ralph, but I know from **SPACE BLASTERS**, sometimes you have to do things you don't want to do for the greater good. Especially when there are bigger enemies you have to think about.

Ralph sullenly walked with me over to the bookshelf. "This is stupid," he said. "What are we going to find in a bunch of old books?"

"Hopefully something useful," I said.

We looked through books for what felt like **FOREVER**. There was a lot about werewolf legends, but not very much practical information.

"How is the zombie research going?" I called out to Regina and Zoe.

They looked up and shook their heads.

"Haven't learned anything new. They are undead, but we already knew that," said Zoe.

"And they like to eat brains," added Regina, scrunching her face up.

"Bernard?" I asked. He had been typing furiously at the computer while we'd been flipping through the old books.

"From what I can tell," he said, still looking at the screen, "zombies and werewolves have a similar attack style. They either eat you, or they bite you, and turn you into one of them."

Regina looked a bit pale.

"Well, now that we know the history of zombies and werewolves, do we have any idea

on how to face an *actual* zombie werewolf?"
Ralph asked, sounding bored. But I saw that
he was drumming his fingers on the table and
his leg was shaking, so I suspected he wasn't
as calm as he was trying to look. This was
something I understood.

"Well," I said. "We did see that werewolves
don't like silver. It can protect you against
them."

"Nothing can protect you against zombies,"
Zoe said glumly. "You just have to run away
from them."

"Not a problem for you then," said Bernard.
"Since you're the fastest out of all of us."

"Wait!" I said, suddenly remembering
something. "One time, on SPACE BLASTERS,
they came up against zombie aliens! And you

know what defeated them? **WATER!**"

I grinned.

"What if zombie aliens are different from zombie werewolves?" said Regina.

"How sure are you that it *is* a zombie werewolf?" asked Bernard.

It was a good question. I was surprised we hadn't asked it before.

"Because we hear it," Regina said firmly. "It growls and shakes the house."

"Wouldn't it only be a werewolf during the full moon?" asked Zoe.

"Good point, General Zoe," I said.

Regina shook her head. "Not a zombie werewolf," she said. "Think about it, if it was a zombie werewolf, it would be a werewolf all the time."

We all nodded. That made sense.

"Maybe it should just *stay* in your basement," suggested Bernard in a small voice. "What if we accidentally let it out? Wouldn't that be worse?"

We all stared at each other. I hadn't thought of that.

"If you are all too scared to come with me, I understand," said Regina. " But Ralph and I haven't been able to sleep for **WEEKS**. We've suspected about the zombie werewolf for ages, but recently it has got **MUCH** louder. We think it is getting angrier. And hungrier. I have to know for sure what is down there."

"I'm not too scared!" I said quickly.

"And who knows," said Zoe. "It might be a

friendly zombie werewolf. Like… a giant puppy or something!"

Ralph snorted. "Yeah, a giant undead puppy that wants to eat our brains."

"It was just a suggestion," Zoe said loudly.

"Nobody has to go down there who doesn't want to," I said. "But there is safety in numbers." I stuck out my hand. "I'm in."

"Me too," said Regina, smiling at me and putting her hand in as well.

"From a scientific perspective, I'll admit, I'm very curious," said Bernard, putting his hand in.

"Obviously I'm not going to let you go down there without me," said Zoe.

"Commander Ralph?" I said.

"Well, it's my house, isn't it?" he said, and

half-heartedly stuck his hand in with all of ours.

"We can do this!" I said, even though I wasn't really sure we could. But **Captain Jane** always says part of being a good Captain is putting on a brave face even if you don't always feel brave. "For the universe!"

'For the universe!'

everyone shouted, flinging their hands in the air.

And right then, a low howl came up from beneath us, and the floorboards started shaking.

"Is that..." said Bernard, who had turned

paler than I'd ever seen him.

Regina nodded.

"That's the zombie werewolf."

CHAPTER 7

SILVER AND SQUIRT GUNS

We all stared at each other.

"Now what do we do?" said Bernard. "We've done all the possible research."

"I still don't feel ready to face a zombie werewolf," Regina admitted.

"We have to see what we're dealing with," I said seriously. "Right now, there are too many unknowns! We don't know how big it is. We don't even know if there are more than one."

"More than one?" Regina yelped. "I'd never

even thought of that!"

"There is a lot we don't know," I said. "Our first step has to be going into the basement to do some surveillance.[7] And then we can come up with a plan on what we want to do with it."

"But we still can't just stroll down unprepared!" said Ralph. "We would have done that ages ago if it was as easy as that."

"Hmm," I said. I hated to admit it, but he had a point. And then, inspiration struck! "We also need what every brave hero needs when he goes on an adventure."

"Or she," said Zoe.

I nodded. "But what IS that?" I asked.

Ralph groaned. "Now is not the time for twenty questions," he said. "Just tell us."

---

[7] Surveillance is a fancy word for spying. Like when on **SPACE BLASTERS**, **Spaceman Jack** will arrive on an alien planet with a disguise so he can scope out any bad guys or threats.

I ignored him. "Think! What makes Batman Batman? What does Wonder Woman have when she fights bad guys? Or Ghost Busters?"

"The Batmobile? An invisible plane? Where are we going to get those?"

I shook my head and looked at Bernard and Zoe. "What about **Spaceman Jack** on **SPACE BLASTERS**?"

Bernard scratched his head. "I don't know, Sam," he said.

"Can we **PLEASE** get back to the zombie werewolf?" said Ralph.

"Special protective gear!" I said. "Batman has his suit, WonderWoman has her amulets, the Ghost Busters have their uniforms. And **Spaceman Jack** has his space suit!"

Everyone just stared at me. I sighed.

"We need Zombie Werewolf Protective Gear!" I explained.

"And where are we going to find that?" said Ralph.

I gestured up and around. "Your house is huge! I'm sure you'll have everything we need. We know that werewolves don't like silver, for example. Regina, do your parents have any silver?"

Regina nodded. "Lots!"

"And I saw that suit of armour when we came in. Do you think we could maybe use that?"

Regina nodded again, more excitedly this time.

"And, remember when I said that water

defeated the zombie aliens on

SPACE BLASTERS? Do you have any squirt

guns? Or water bottles?"

"Of course we have squirt guns," said Ralph.

"I have the Squirt Master XL," he said smugly.

Of course he did. The Squirt Master XL is only the **BEST** squirt gun money can buy.

"I actually have two," he added. "One for each hand."

"Well, in this case, two for multiple people," said Zoe. "I'll be taking one of those, thank you very much. I always win my neighbourhood squirt-gun battles."

It's true. I've seen her in action.

"Okay," said Bernard, scribbling furiously in his notebook. "We have silver and squirt guns, the suit of armour...what else do we need?"

"Flashlights," I said decisively. "Flashlights **ALWAYS** come in handy."

"You're just saying that because you are afraid of the dark," said Ralph with a sneer.

"I think I proved when we went camping that

I most definitely am **NOT** afraid of the dark,"
I said. "And another thing I always find useful,
for any mission, is poison mist."

"But where are we going to find poison
mist?" Regina wailed. "Our mission is doomed!"

Ralph rolled his eyes. "Sam is talking about
hairspray."

"Which doubles as poison
mist!" I said. "Who would
want hairspray sprayed
in their eyes and
mouth? It's extremely
effective."

"Fine, I'll admit it might
be useful for temporarily blinding
a zombie werewolf," said Ralph. "And our mum
definitely has some."

"I think we should bring down some tennis balls or something," said Zoe. "Just in case it acts like a dog. We never know."

"That's genius!" said Bernard. "I like your reasoning. It makes perfect sense that the zombie werewolf might act like a dog." Then he paused. "But what do we do if it *doesn't* act like a dog?"

"If it doesn't want to play fetch, we can pelt it with the tennis balls!" said Regina, who sounded alarmingly excited about this possibility.

"We should probably bring some rope or a net too," said Ralph. "In case we need to tie it down."

"Who is going to get close enough to do that?" said Bernard.

Everyone looked at me. "We'll deal with that when we get to it," I said quickly. "First we need to get all our supplies, and our special protective gear."

Suddenly, Regina gasped. "I just remembered something!" she said. "It's locked! The basement!"

"Mum and Dad also said under **NO CIRCUMSTANCES** are we allowed to go down there," Ralph added.

"Well…maybe that's for the best?" said Bernard, looking a bit relieved. "Like I said earlier, maybe it is trapped down there for a *reason*. Probably a very good reason. Like keeping something scary trapped inside. Maybe we should keep that door locked." He glanced over at me.

Part of me agreed with Bernard. A pretty big part. But another part of me knew we couldn't give up. Not when we'd promised we'd help. And a promise is important. Plus, Ralph would never let me live it down if I let my fear get the best of me.

I took a deep breath. "We've come too far to give up now," I said, even though technically we hadn't done very much yet. But **Captain Jane** always says that when her crew wants to turn back.

Bernard gave a resigned sigh. "I guess you are right."

I turned to Ralph and Regina and asked the obvious question.

"Do you know where the key is?"

Regina nodded. "It'll be in my parents'

bedroom. We'll have to go in there any way to get some of my mum's silver jewellery."

"Okay," I said, nodding seriously. I turned to Bernard. "Can you write this down? First step of our mission is to gather our supplies and find the key. Second step is to put on our protective gear. Third step is to go down into the basement to do our surveillance."

"Is the fourth step being eaten by a zombie werewolf?" said Ralph. I couldn't tell if he was kidding or not.

"That is definitely **NOT** the fourth step," I said. "As soon as we know what we are dealing with, we'll come back up to the house, lock the door again behind us, and make stage two of our plan." I looked up at the grandfather clock in the corner of the library.

"We might have to save stage two for another time though. Because my dad is coming to get us after dinner."

"Easy for you to say," said Regina. "You don't have to sleep in a house with a zombie werewolf in the basement."

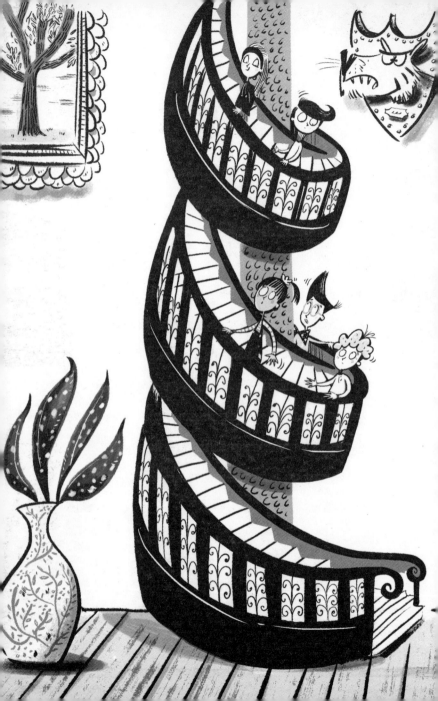

CHAPTER 8

CROWNS IN THE CLOSET

We followed Ralph and Regina out of the library and up another spiral staircase.

"Do you ever get lost in here?" asked Bernard, his mouth a little open.

"Of course not," said Ralph snootily. "We know every corner of this house."

"Except the basement," said Regina.

We got to the top of the staircase and turned down a dark corridor. All the curtains were closed, and it was hard to see far ahead of us. The ground was covered in thick carpets, making our footsteps almost impossible to hear.

"What's that . . . smell?" said Zoe, wrinkling her nose.

Ralph and Regina stopped and we all took big sniffs.

"That's just what this wing of the house smells like," said Regina. "I've never really noticed it before."

"It kind of smells like wet dog," said Zoe. And then she looked embarrassed, like she realized she'd just said something rude. "But not in a bad way! I like the smell of dogs!"

"We don't have a dog," said Regina.

I immediately thought of the zombie werewolf again, but kept that thought to myself.

At the end of the hall, we went into another

dark room. In the middle was a **HUGE** bed with curtains all around it. It was like its own small room.

"This way," whispered Regina, pointing in the corner where there was a big dresser under a mirror and then what looked like a wardrobe. "The key will be in the top drawer, and the silver jewellery will be there too. There might be more in the wardrobe."

We crept over to the dresser, and Regina pulled open the top drawer.

It was like opening a treasure chest! It was filled with sparkling earrings and gold necklaces and diamond rings.

"The key should be in here somewhere," said Regina, sticking her tongue out in concentration as she dug around the drawer,

tossing necklaces and rings out behind her.
"Take anything that looks like it might be
silver," she said.

"Can I wear this just because I like it?" said
Zoe, putting on a gigantic diamond necklace.
Bernard was wearing a string of pearls around
his head like a crown.

"Sure," said Regina, sounding distracted.
"But remember to have some silver too!"

"Are you sure your parents won't mind?" said Bernard, putting a silver ring on his thumb. He tossed me a silver necklace that I put around my neck.

"They aren't going to find out," said Ralph. "We're going to sneak down there, remember? And then we'll put everything back before they notice."

"Unless we get eaten by the zombie werewolf," said Zoe.

"Well, then we'll have bigger problems," said Ralph.

"Ah-ha! I found the key!" Regina cried, holding it up. She looked us all over. "Hmm. I think we probably need more silver."

"We've still got the suit of armour too," I said. I was hoping to wear the helmet from that.

"It's still good to get as much as we can up here," Regina said. "Let's check out the wardrobe. That's where my parents keep the *really* good stuff."

It was a big wardrobe, but with all five of us in there, it felt a little cramped. Something **FURRY** rubbed up against my arm.

"**ARGH!**"

"Calm down, Sam," said Ralph, "it's just a coat." He flipped a light switch and I saw that there were a LOT of fur coats around us.

"Your mum sure likes fur," I said, swallowing. I didn't say what else I was thinking (who better to have fur coats than a **WEREWOLF!**).

"There should be something good up here," said Regina, pointing at a shelf above us. "Give me a boost up."

We all crouched and put our hands together to make a step and lifted her up. She rummaged around above us for a moment.

"Hurry up!" said Ralph, "my hand hurts!"

"Just a second," she said. "I've got it!" She hopped off our hands, clutching something silver and shiny.

"Is that a **CROWN**?" said Zoe with a gasp.

"It's my mum's tiara," said Regina. "She wears it to parties sometimes." She balanced it on top of her head. "And it's all silver! Perfect protection against werewolves."

Something occurred to me. If Ralph and Regina's parents were werewolves, like I was starting to suspect, why would they have all this silver? It didn't make sense. Something wasn't adding up. Unless they had the silver to trick people into thinking they *weren't* werewolves?! I was going to have to pay extra-close attention to solve this one.

ᕦ∕ᕤ

After we'd all covered ourselves in silver, we went back downstairs. Ralph found tennis balls, a flashlight, and an old fishing net in a storage cupboard, and Regina grabbed her mum's hairspray from the bathroom. We filled both Squirt Master XLs with water. All that was left was the suit of armour.

It came apart surprisingly easily, but was heavier than I thought it would be. We each took a piece of it.

"I get the helmet," said Ralph, grabbing it. "After all, it's my suit of armour."

Zoe rolled her eyes.

"Your house, your rules," I said. I ended up with the chest plate, which I was pretty happy about. And I also had a silver necklace and one of the Squirt Master XLs.

When we were all ready, we stood in front of a giant mirror in the front room to make sure we had everything we needed for our mission.

"We look…" I paused, trying to find the right word.

"Awesome," said Bernard, adjusting the knee plates that he'd taken from the suit of armour.

"Ridiculous," said Ralph with a snort.

"Expensive," said Zoe, admiring her diamond necklace.

"Amazing!" added Regina.

"We look ready," I said firmly.

Ready to face whatever was in the basement.

CHAPTER 9

DOWN BELOW

We crept as quietly as we could to the back
of the house, where the basement door was.
But with all of our gear on, it was hard not to
make a lot of noise. Especially with everyone
clanking around in their piece of armour.

"Good thing your parents aren't in the
house," said Bernard, between heavy breaths.
"They'd definitely hear us."

And then we were at the door to the
basement. The **LOCKED** door. Regina
stepped forward, key in hand, and paused. She
looked over her shoulder at us.

"Everyone ready?" she asked.

"Who is going down first?" said Bernard.

We all looked at each other.

"Aren't you supposed to be the brave one?"
Ralph said to me with a smirk. "You're our
fearless Captain, aren't you?"

"It's our basement," said Regina. "I'll go first."

"I'll be right next to you," I said. I didn't

want anyone thinking I was too scared to go down into the basement. I looked at Ralph.

"Commander Ralph, can you bring up the rear? You'll be in charge of making sure we don't accidentally get locked in. It's your house, so you'll know how the doors work."

Ralph went a little pale. He didn't seem so smug any more.

"That's a good idea," said Regina. "Right, Ralph?"

"Er, right," said Ralph.

"That means General Zoe and Chief Research Officer Bernard go behind me," I said. "Now, before we go down there, we need a code word in case things go wrong."

"What about **WOOF WOOF WOOF**?" said Zoe.

"I like it!" Regina said.

"Okay," I said, trying to figure out how to stall for more time and not coming up with anything. "I guess this is it. Zoe, do you have the tennis balls?" Zoe nodded. "Bernard, do you have the hairspray?" Bernard held it out. "Ralph, you've got your Squirt Master XL?" Ralph waved it around in the air. "Great, I've got the other one. That just leaves the flashlight and the net." I looked up at Regina. She was holding the flashlight in one hand, and the net was thrown over her shoulder.

"I've got it," she said determinedly.

"Then here we go. We'll follow you," I said.

We all held our breath as she put the key in the lock and turned. The door opened with a slow creak, showing a long dark staircase.

"Last chance to turn back," I whispered.

"For the universe!"[8] Bernard whispered back.

And Regina turned on her flashlight, and led us down below.

Zoe noticed the smell first.

"It's back! The wet dog smell! And stronger down here!" she said.

"Maybe that is what zombie werewolves smell like," I whispered back.

"Be quiet!" hissed Ralph. "We're trying to sneak up on it, aren't we?"

We had to go very slowly, because we were all in single file. Just as we were almost at the bottom of the stairs, there was a loud **CLANK**, followed by another one. Then something tumbled past me on the stairs.

"What was *that*?" I gasped.

---

[8] This is the signature saying on SPACE BLASTERS. My friends and I say it anytime we are about to do something AWESOME or a little scary.

CLANK CLANK CLANK

"I think it is one of my armour knees!" said Bernard, sounding panicked. "It just fell off! Now my knee isn't protected!"

"Who cares about your knee?" said Ralph. "Now the zombie werewolf will definitely be awake!"

"Be quiet!" Regina hissed.

And then I heard it. A low howl, followed by a gurgle and a growl. As my eyes adjusted to the dark, I saw **HUGE FURRY SHAPES EVERYWHERE**.

"**IT'S A ZOMBIE WEREWOLF ARMY!**" I shouted, before I could stop myself. "Zoe! Throw your tennis balls! Ralph! Fire your squirt master!"

Behind me, I heard Zoe yelp. "Not at me!" she said. "Down into the basement!"

A tennis ball hit me on the head and bounced into the basement.

"**THEY ARE GETTING CLOSER!**" Bernard cried out. "**THE SILVER ISN'T WORKING!**"

I don't know how he saw what was happening in the dark with just the one beam of light from Regina's flashlight waving around, but I believed him.

And then I saw the gleam of a beady eye and a long snout.

"RETREAT! RETREAT!" I shouted.

WOOF!

WOOF!

WOOF!

Before I turned, I shot my Squirt Master XL into the dark, hoping it would get a zombie werewolf or two.

We ran up the stairs, not caring how much noise we made now, and as soon as we were all out, Ralph slammed the door shut, and Regina locked it.

"I can still hear them!" Zoe's eyes were huge. "We have to get out of here!"

"What if the door can't hold them?" wailed Bernard. "We need to put something against it!"

"Quick!" I said, taking off my chest plate. "Pile up your armour in front of the door! The silver will keep them from breaking through." I had no idea if this was actually the case but it was the only idea I had.

Everyone threw their armour in a heap at the base of the door.

The grumbling, growling, groaning noises had stopped.

We all stared at each other.

"Let's…go back in the kitchen," I said. I didn't want to be anywhere near the basement door.

We got back to the kitchen and all collapsed into chairs, breathing heavily like we'd just run a race.

"That was close," said Regina finally. "I'm glad you guys were with us though. There's no way Ralph and I could have survived that on our own! We would have been zombie food for sure!"

"Or zombie-*fied*," said Bernard. "If they decided to turn you into zombies instead of eating you."

"Regina," I said seriously. "There isn't just one zombie werewolf in your basement. There is a whole **ARMY**."

CHAPTER 10

QUAIL, SQUAB AND PIGEON

After everyone had caught their breath, we took off all our protective gear and put it back where we'd found it.

Now that I'd seen what was in the basement, I had a new theory about Ralph and Regina's parents.

"Regina," I said. "I think your parents might be zombie-werewolf **HUNTERS!**"

It made perfect sense. Why they had so much silver. Why they had so much fur. (I wondered if the fur coats were werewolf skins!) And most importantly, why they insisted the basement was off limits.

Regina laughed. "Sam," she said, "my mum and dad both have regular jobs. My dad works at a bank and my mum works with art."

I shook my head. "Those might be their day jobs, but they are definitely also zombie-werewolf hunters. How else do you explain everything in your house? And most of all, everything in the basement! They are using your basement as a zombie werewolf cage!"

Bernard's eyes lit up. "Maybe they are keeping them locked up because they are working with a scientist who is going to turn them back into humans!"

Ralph snorted. "That is ridiculous. Like something in a movie."

Zoe put her hands on her hips. "What is your explanation then?" she said.

Ralph looked a little startled. "I . . . I . . . I don't know," he admitted. "But you are all right about one thing. We really *do* have an army of zombie werewolves in our basement."

"I think we should ask your parents about it," said Zoe. "Tonight. At dinner."

Ralph and Regina exchanged a look. "I don't know," said Regina. Then she sighed. "But we can try."

❧

Dinner at the Zinkermans was very different from dinner at my house. We ate in what Ralph and Regina called their 'formal dining room'. Like the rest of their house, it was super fancy and old fashioned. There were tall candlesticks all down the long table, more forks than I knew what to do with, and behind our chairs, giant paintings of old people looked down at us.

"Who is that?" I asked Regina as we were sitting down, pointing at the grumpy looking man in the painting directly behind me. I felt like he was staring at me. It was creepy.

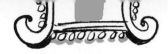

"That's Great-Great Uncle Archibald," she said. "He was a sea captain."

I was impressed despite myself.

Ralph and Regina's parents came in, wearing all black and looking like spies. They always did, but now I wondered if that was also what secret zombie-werewolf hunters looked like. I wondered if they would teach me how to be a zombie-werewolf hunter.

"Children!" trilled their mum. "So lovely to have you all over! It's been absolutely ages since Ralphie and Reginie had friends over. And we so love having company."

"Glad to see you all survived . . ." Their dad paused and I took a deep breath. Did he know that we'd been down in the basement? ". . . our recent camping adventure!"

I let out my breath.

"What did you get up to this afternoon?" said Mr Zinkerman.

While I was thinking of the best way to answer this, my stomach let out a loud growl. I hadn't eaten anything since the cookies earlier in the day and I was suddenly starving! Being a zombie-werewolf hunter was hungry work.

I coughed to cover the sound of my growling stomach. But I also wondered if we were going to actually have dinner or if we were just going to sit around the fancy table.

But then a man and a lady, both wearing uniforms, came in carrying platters of food.

The lady put a small bird on my plate.

Zoe poked at the bird on her own plate. "What . . . is this?" she said. "A miniature chicken?"

"It's quail, darling," said Mrs Zinkerman. "A small bird."

"I shot them myself," added Mr Zinkerman.

More proof that they were zombie-werewolf hunters!

"I've never had quail," said Bernard. "But I've had duck before. At Sam's house."

"Is your father a hunting man?" asked Mr Zinkerman.

I shook my head. "We get our duck from the Chinese supermarket." I looked down at the quail. I'd just realized what it reminded me of. "This looks a little bit like pigeon," I said.

"**PIGEON?**" yelped Zoe. "Like the ones on the roof?"

"I've had it in Hong Kong," I explained. "But I don't think they cook the city ones."

"I'd like to try pigeon," said Regina.

"That's my adventurous girl," said Mrs Zinkerman with a smile. She looked over at me. "Do you know," she said, "that squab, which is one of my favourite types of poultry, is a type of pigeon meat? It is quite the delicacy! I'm very impressed. You must have quite a sophisticated palate."

I beamed, and ignored Ralph snorting across from me.

"What do you think of the quail?" she said.

I took a bite. It tasted a little bit like chicken, and a little bit like pigeon. I liked it!

"It's good!" I said.

After I took a few bites, so did Zoe and Bernard.

"He's right," said Bernard, with his mouth a little full. "It is good!"

"I'm glad you like it," whispered Regina. "I was worried you'd think it was weird."

It was funny to think that even though her house was fancy, and our dinner had been served by a butler, Regina was worried about what we'd think of the food! I thought food was just something that I worried about at my house, and it was kind of nice to know other people felt like that too sometimes.

"You'll have to come over another time," said Mrs Zinkerman. And then she sat straight up. "Oh! I've just had the most inspired idea! You all simply must come to the Halloween gala at the museum next weekend!"

"What's a gala?" said Zoe.

"It's just a fancy word for a party," said Regina.

I wasn't surprised that the Zinkermans had fancy words for things.

"It is going to be glorious, oh, you'll all absolutely love it!' said Mrs Zinkerman. "There is a big costume party in the children's wing. I'll let your parents know the details. Would you all like that?"

Ralph and I exchanged a look. It was one thing being forced to go camping together, and for me to come over to his house at Regina's request to help them with their zombie werewolf problem, but going to a

Halloween party together was bordering on 'friend' territory. I wasn't sure how either of us felt about it.

I decided to let him answer first.

Ralph sighed dramatically and then rolled his eyes. "You should come," he said grudgingly, and I was so startled I dropped my fork on the floor.

"Okay," I said.

"Okay?" said Zoe, looking closely at me. Usually we spent Halloween trick-or-treating together.

Regina reached out and squeezed Zoe's hand. "It'll be really fun," she said. "I promise."

"Okay," said Zoe, smiling.

"Okay!" said Bernard.

"Okay then!" said Mrs Zinkerman with a

light laugh. "Then it is all settled. I'll organize the details." She got her phone out and started tapping away at it.

While Mrs Zinkerman was distracted, Zoe caught my eye.

"**THE BASEMENT**," she mouthed.

She was right! In all the excitement about the fancy dinner and the party, I'd somehow almost forgotten about asking about what was in the basement!

But I didn't feel like it was right for me to ask. They were Ralph and Regina's parents after all. And **Spaceman Jack** always says you never drive another crew's spaceship without permission. This was sort of like that.

"Basement?" I whispered as loud as I dared to Regina.

She bit her lip but then cleared her throat. "Mother?" she said. "We were . . . wondering . . . "

As her voice trailed off both her parents looked up.

"Wondering . . . ?" said Mr Zinkerman.

But Regina didn't look like she was feeling brave enough to say it.

"Are there zombie werewolves in your basement?" I blurted.

Mr and Mrs Zinkerman looked at each other and burst out laughing.

"Oh Sam, you really do have the most fantastic imagination. But zombies in the basement! What an idea," said Mrs Zinkerman.

"You didn't try to go down there though, did you?" said Mr Zinkerman, suddenly serious. "Regina, Ralph – you know it is off limits."

This time I kept my mouth zipped shut.
Regina shook her head.

"Philip, it's locked, remember?" said Mrs
Zinkerman. "So even if they were being
naughty," she waggled her finger in our
direction, "they couldn't have got in."

"We did . . . take apart the suit of armour," Ralph suddenly admitted. "We wanted to try it on."

Mr Zinkerman let out an unexpected, big booming laugh. "Well, that is certainly all right. That thing has been through plenty of battles."

I wondered if he wore it when he went hunting zombie werewolves! Because now I was EXTRA-convinced that they were zombie-werewolf hunters.[9]

---

[9] Why else would there be a zombie werewolf army in the basement?

CHAPTER 11

NA-NA THE PUMPKIN

We didn't have a chance to make a new plan because right after dinner, my dad came to pick up me, Zoe and Bernard.

"What *do* you say to Mr and Mrs Zinkerman?" he prompted before we got into the car.

"Thank you!" we said, waving up at where they were standing in the doorway.

"Well," my dad said as we pulled away. "That is certainly an impressive house. Did you have a nice time?"

We all nodded. Because we couldn't exactly explain that we'd discovered an army of zombie werewolves in the basement and suspected that Mr and Mrs Zinkerman were secret zombie-werewolf hunters, could we?

After we dropped off Zoe and Bernard and went home, I ran up to my room to write **EVERYTHING** down in my special adventure notebook so I wouldn't forget a single thing. I started doing this after we became spider catchers. I figured with all the adventures we were having, I needed to record it. Just in case anyone asked for proof of how brave I was.

Every day that week, we asked Ralph and
Regina if there were any updates on the
zombie werewolf situation.

"There is still so much we don't know!" said
Regina one day at lunch. She *and* Ralph had
started sitting with us, which was both weird
and nice. She started listing things off on
her fingers. "Are my parents actually zombie-
werewolf hunters? Do they even know what
is down there? Are we safe? Is the zombie
werewolf army just getting stronger?" She
touched her hand to her silver necklace. "I've
been wearing this just in case, but I don't
know how well it works."

These were all very good points.

"And you're still hearing the zombie

werewolf sounds at night?" I asked.

Both Ralph and Regina nodded.

"They keep getting louder," Ralph said. "And yesterday we heard a bang, and now there is a hole in the bottom of the door!"

"It's too small for a zombie werewolf to get through," said Regina quickly, "but it won't be long till they break the door down!"

"We're going to have to come up with a new plan," I said. Then I asked something that had been on my mind since we went to their house. "Do you think your parents would teach us how to be zombie-werewolf hunters? You know, if that's what they actually are."

Ralph snorted. "You aren't brave enough to be a zombie-werewolf hunter," he said. "That is only for the **BRAVEST** people."

Before I could defend myself, Regina jumped

in. "Of course Sam is brave enough to be a zombie-werewolf hunter! He's the bravest person I know!" She paused and then grinned. "Other than myself, of course."

"I think we are all brave enough to be zombie-werewolf hunters," I said. I looked at Zoe and Bernard. "It's probably the next logical step after everything else we've done. Just think of all the certificates we'll have!"

"I'll have to think about it," said Zoe, taking a bite of her sandwich. "I might want to be a racecar driver. Or a fire fighter."

"You can probably do all of those things," I said matter-of-factly. "I'm going to be an astronaut **AND** a zombie-werewolf hunter."

"I'll be a zombie-werewolf hunter but only if I'm in charge of the research," said Bernard.

"That is probably okay," I said.

"This is ridiculous!" burst out Ralph. "We don't even know if that is a real job!"

"Of course we do," I said. "It's your parents' **SECRET** job!"

Ralph just shook his head and took a sip of his milk.

"By the way," said Regina, "I can't wait to go to your house this weekend, Sam!"

I almost spit out my juice. "What?" I said. I hadn't heard anything about this! Even though Ralph and I weren't total enemies right now, it didn't mean I wanted him coming over to my **HOUSE!** Or Regina, even though she was so nice. What if Na-Na fell asleep on the couch and started snoring in front of them? Or if my dad cooked something smelly? Or Lucy asked them embarrassing questions? It would be a complete and utter **DISASTER**. Ralph would never let me hear the end of it.

"Didn't your parents tell you?" said Regina. "Our parents have to go over early to the museum to help set up, so we are coming over to your house first and all going over together. It will be the perfect opportunity for us to come up with a new plan!" She beamed like this was the best plan instead of the **WORST** one. "And if we decide we need to do more research, a museum is the **PERFECT** place for that," she went on.

I couldn't argue with her there. I managed a smile. "Great!" I said.

At least Zoe and Bernard would be there too.

JUST KEEP SMILING

I was nervous the rest of the week. Not only were Ralph and Regina coming over to my house, we were going to have to come up with a new plan to face the zombie werewolves. The whole thing made my stomach hurt.

The only thing that helped was putting up Halloween decorations. I had to **BEG** my mum to put them up (she says they just make a mess) but finally she said yes, as long as I promised to help clean them up afterwards.

I didn't just want decorations outside the house. I wanted them everywhere! Na-Na, who loves *all* holidays, helped me. We hung up fake spider webs across every doorway. We left monster masks hiding in *every* corner.

And she even ordered ghost balloons
for us to hang from the ceiling.

∽ ∾

Zoe arrived first that evening. She was
dressed as a pirate and looked **AMAZING!**

I told her so.

I was dressed as what I always dress up as.
Spaceman Jack from SPACE BLASTERS. Ever
since I started watching SPACE BLASTERS,
I've dressed up as **Spaceman Jack** every chance
I get.

Bernard arrived next. He was dressed as a
T-Rex.

"You look **AWESOME!**" I said, giving him a
high-five.

Lucy ran in to show us her costume. She
wasn't going to the party with us; she was

going trick-or-treating with our parents. She was dressed as a lion. She had also put a lion's mane around her cat Butterbutt, who did not seem especially pleased by this.

"I'm the leader of the pride!" Lucy said, with a big roar. Butterbutt yowled along with her.

Of course, right at this moment, when Lucy was roaring and Butterbutt was yowling, Ralph and Regina showed up.

Ralph was dressed up as a vampire, and I

could tell that he had a fancy store-bought costume instead of a homemade one like mine. He had on a long black cape with a high collar and even his vampire face make-up looked like it had been professionally done! I was very impressed despite myself.

"I love all your decorations!" said Regina, looking round. She was dressed as a butterfly with **HUGE** blue and green wings. Both Lucy and Butterbutt were very interested in the wings. Butterbutt kept pawing at them and Lucy tried to wrap herself in one of them.

"These are so shiny!" she said.

Regina just laughed. "You can borrow my costume when you are big enough to fit in it," she said.

"Really?" asked Lucy, eyes bright.

"Really," said Regina.

Lucy turned to Ralph with a sneaky Lucy grin. "I like **YOUR** cape too. Can I borrow that one day as well?"

Ralph looked a little bit panicked by my ferocious-looking little sister ambushing him. "Umm. Sure," he said.

"**HOORAY!**" shouted Lucy, so loud that it made us all jump.

"Where's your pet snake?" Regina asked, looking around the room like Fang might be anywhere.

"Up in my room," I said. "Because he's so dangerous, we have to keep him upstairs."

"And away from Butterbutt," said Lucy. "Butterbutt loves Fang. I think they might be best friends."

"Can we see him?" asked Regina.

I didn't really want to show Ralph and Regina my room because I was worried they might make fun of it, but I didn't know how to get out of it.

"Okay," I said. "Follow me."

My room felt extra cramped with all of us

in there, especially because Lucy came in too.
And Butterbutt.

Fang was curled up on a rock in his cage, but he sat up when he sensed us.

"Whoa," said Ralph, taking a step back. "You sleep in here with a snake?"

I nodded proudly. "I sure do," I said.

"Can we get him out?" asked Regina, sounding excited. "Maybe he can help us! Do you think snakes eat zombie werewolves?"

I shook my head. "He can get pretty ferocious, and he's not like a dog that just does what you tell him to do. I wouldn't want him getting confused and trying to eat one of us."

"That makes sense," said Regina, putting her face up next to Fang's cage. "It's pretty impressive that you have a man-eating snake as a pet!"

I just nodded. Even though I'd never technically seen Fang eat anything bigger than a very small mouse. He *might* still be a man-eating snake, after all.

Ralph was looking around my room at all my **SPACE BLASTERS** gear on the walls. "Is this from that show you are always talking about?" he said.

I nodded.

"It actually looks pretty cool," he said, looking up at a poster of **Spaceman Jack** and his alien friend Five-Eyed Frank. "Maybe I'll check it out."

"Maybe one day we can all watch SPACE BLASTERS together," I said. "We can start with the very first episode, so you can catch up."

"Yeah!" said Zoe.

"I'd love that!" said Regina.

Ralph shrugged. "Maybe."

❧ ❧

After my parents had insisted on taking about a **GAZILLION** pictures of us all dressed up, we got into our mini-van. Na-Na was driving us to the museum because my parents were taking Lucy trick-or-treating.

Na-Na was dressed as a giant pumpkin. She'd even painted her face orange and spray-painted her hair green.

"That's your *grandma*?" said Ralph,

his eyes wide. "I didn't know grandmas dressed up for Halloween."

"Mine does," I said proudly. "She's the best."

"We haven't made a new plan!" Regina whispered as we climbed into the mini-van, sounding panicked.

"That's okay," I said. "We can come up with something at the museum! We'll definitely have a new plan by the end of the night."

"Do you promise?" said Regina, her eyes wide.

"I promise," I said.

Behind me, Bernard groaned. "Sam, you have to stop making promises without consulting us first."

CHAPTER 12

KEEP IT CASUAL

If I hadn't just seen Ralph and Regina's house, I would have said the Central Museum was the **FANCIEST** building I'd ever seen. It was still pretty fancy. It had marble columns in the front and giant statues of lions welcoming us and a big staircase leading to a huge doorway. My favourite museum was still the Space Museum[10] but this one might have been my second favourite. And I hadn't even been inside yet!

"Whoa," I said.

---

[10] Because I love everything about space. Obviously.

"We're going here for the Halloween party?" squeaked Zoe.

Na-Na squinted up at the building. "I hope so," she said. "I'm not driving you anywhere else. I've got to get back to pass out candy and watch my shows."

"She means she's got to get back to eat candy," I whispered to Bernard, but not quietly enough.

"I heard that," said Na-Na, and Bernard flushed bright red. But Na-Na was smiling. "If you're lucky, I'll save you some candy. Now get out and go to your fancy party! Have fun!"

～～

Once we were inside the museum, we were welcomed by a lady in a cat costume.

"Welcome to our annual Halloween Bash!"

she said. "Children, follow me this way. Your party is in this room to the left. In the Dinosaur Room!"

"**COOL!**" said Bernard, hopping up and down in his T-Rex costume. "That's my favourite room in the museum! My dad takes me there all the time!"

We followed the cat lady into a **GIGANTIC** room filled with dinosaur skeletons! I couldn't believe it. This was the kind of thing Bernard's dad[11] dug up.

The long neck is my favourite," I said, pointing at it. It was full length and took up almost the whole room.

"That's called a brontosaurus," said Bernard.

Next to the long neck was a huge T-Rex,

---

[11] Bernard's dad is a paleontologist, which means he studies super-old things like really old rocks with leaves stuck in them.

with its mouth wide open so we could see all its teeth.

The room would have been pretty exciting with just the dinosaurs, but there were also Halloween decorations everywhere. Even more than Na-Na and I had put up in our house.

Spider webs hung from the dinosaur bones and there were long tables stretching out beside the dinosaurs with candy and fruit punch. For a second, I was so amazed by it all that I forgot about our zombie werewolf problem.

"This is the best party I've ever been to!" said Zoe.

Regina beamed. "I'm so glad you guys are here!" she said. "Come on, let's go and get some candy. Last year, they had FULL SIZE candy bars and you could just take as many as you wanted." Then she started to giggle. "Ralph ate too many all at once and threw up in the bushes outside."

Ralph turned red under his vampire make-up.

"Happens to the best of us," I said.

As we were walking towards one of the tables covered in candy, Bernard suddenly grabbed my arm. "Sam! Look!"

I looked where he was pointing. All I saw was a sign for other exhibits in the museum.

"What is it?" I said.

"**MUMMIES!**"

"What about mummies?"

"The museum has a whole section on mummies!"

I frowned. "Since when are you so interested in mummies?"

"Think about it, Sam. Mummies are **BASICALLY** zombies, but wrapped in cloth. What better place to do zombie research than here in the museum? It's perfect!"

Everything clicked into place. I grabbed Bernard by the shoulders, which was hard to do under his T-Rex costume.

"Bernard!" I exclaimed. "You're a genius!"

He grinned. "I know," he said happily.

I quickly told the others about our discovery. I just knew we'd have to find something in the museum that could help us defeat the zombie werewolf army. And if we didn't . . . Well, I didn't like thinking about that.

"Before we go looking in the mummy exhibit, can we have some candy?" said Zoe, unwrapping a chocolate bar.

She seemed slightly less concerned than I was about how urgently we needed to figure out a plan. But I nodded.

"Of course," I said. "It is important to fuel up before a mission." Then I lowered my voice. "And we're going to have to figure out a plan to sneak out of this room and into the mummy exhibit without any of the grown-ups noticing. We're going to have to act casual."

"What do you mean act casual?" said Ralph.

"Not suspicious," I said. "Like this." I put my hands in my pockets and whistled as I walked very slowly in a circle. "You know, casual."

Regina burst out laughing. "Sam! You don't ever do that. I think we should just wait till they are distracted and then walk very fast out of the room."

"I like Regina's plan," said Zoe, her mouth full of chocolate.

"It's basically the same as my plan," I said, feeling slightly defensive. Then I looked around and noticed that the grown-ups were busy putting out more candy on a table across the room. "Now is our chance! Quick! Walk casually!"

We all walked as quickly and casually as we could. Ralph was rolling his eyes, but he always does that so it worked perfectly.

And then we were out of the dinosaur room and in a dark corridor. I blinked, trying to see more clearly. "I wish we had a flashlight," I said.

"Too bad your costume doesn't come with one," smirked Ralph, rapping me on my SPACE BLASTERS helmet.

"Bernard, which way was the mummy exhibit?" said Zoe.

Bernard looked around. "That way, I think? There aren't any signs in here."

"Well, we might as well try that way," I said. "Everyone stay together, this place is **HUGE**. And remember, our emergency call is still **WOOF-WOOF-WOOF**."

We crept along the corridor, staying as close as we could. I could feel my hands starting to sweat.

Then we turned a corner and entered another big room. There were a few lights on in the corners, so it wasn't as dark as the hallway, but it wasn't brightly lit either.

"Is this the mummy room?" whispered Zoe.

"It can't be," said Bernard. "I can't see a single mummy."

"I know this room!" said Regina suddenly. "It's the rare gem room. It's one of my favourites! Come and look at this!" She led us over to one of the display cases in the middle of the room.

I peered over her shoulder and gasped.

CHAPTER 13

MUMMIES AND MARTIAN ROCKS

There was a **HUGE** ruby, practically the size of my head, sparkling under the dim lights.

"Whoa," I said.

"And look at these," Regina said, pulling me towards another display case. This one was filled with sparkly white crystals. "But I bet I know which gem will be your favourite." She pointed at a big case up against a wall.

I went over to it and frowned. Inside

was just a big grey rock. It didn't look that exciting. Especially compared to the ruby and the crystals.

"Read the description," Regina said. "Trust me, you're going to **LOVE** it."

I looked over at the sign.

RARE MARTIAN METEORITE
This is a piece of a meteorite from Mars and was formed approximately 4.4 billion years ago

"**THIS ROCK IS FROM MARS?**" I yelled. I couldn't believe it. It was the closest I'd ever been to real space! Or an alien!

"Keep it down!" hissed Ralph. "Casual, remember? It's just a rock."

But I was too excited to stay casual.

"A ROCK FROM MARS!" I said. "IT IS
BASICALLY AN ALIEN ROCK!"

Bernard rushed over and pressed his face
to the glass. "Wow," he said.

RARE MARTIAN
METEORITE

"Guys, we aren't here to do space research, remember?" said Zoe. "We can come back to the museum to look at the space rock. Right now we have to find the mummy exhibit so we can make a plan. We're running out of time!"

I pulled myself away from the martian rock. "You're right," I said, nodding. "Sorry team, I got a little distracted there."

"Told you that you would like it," said Regina. "But Zoe's right, we have to keep going. Who knows what the zombie werewolf army will get up to with all of us out of the house? And look!" She pointed up at a sign in the corner. "The mummy exhibit is right through there!"

As we left the gem room, I looked back at the martian rock one last time.

☙ ❧

The corridor leading to the mummy exhibit was even darker than the first one. And as we made our way through it, I started to hear a low, thumping sound.

I stopped short, and Ralph ran into me.

"Hey!" he said.

"Shh!" I said. "Listen!"

Everyone else stopped too.

"Do you hear that?" I said.

"Hear what?" said Ralph.

"That . . . thumping noise. You have to really listen."

I could almost feel it more than hear it, like it was coming up from the ground.

"I hear it," said Bernard, looking a little panicked.

"I hear something else too," said Zoe, tilting

her head to the side. "Voices, maybe?"

"Maybe we've gone in a circle," said Regina, frowning. "And we've gone back to the party."

"I don't think so," I said.

"This place is like a maze," said Ralph. "I still don't know my way around and I've been here lots."

I made a decision. "Let's just keep going," I said. "But stay together."

The sounds were getting louder as we kept going down the corridor.

"Sam," said Zoe, "maybe we should turn back."

"We're almost there," I said. "We can't give up now."

We reached the end of the corridor and turned a corner. The noise was really loud now.

The first thing I saw was a huge mummy staring down at me from a glass case on the wall.

THEN I SAW THE ZOMBIES.

CHAPTER 14

ZOMBIE ATTACK!

There were zombies everywhere!

Some had green melting faces, some had gaping holes in their heads, and ALL of them looked like they wanted to EAT US. There was a strange purple light over all of them and that strange thumping was louder than ever.

We all stood, frozen, trying to figure out what we were seeing.

"**WOOF-WOOF-WOOF**," Bernard whispered frantically. "**WOOF-WOOF!**"

Then one of the zombies **LOOKED**

STRAIGHT AT ME AND STARTED COMING TOWARDS US.

My Captain instincts kicked in. "RUN!" I shouted, turning back down the corridor.

We all ran as fast as we could. Zoe was at the front, but she kept looking back to make sure we were right behind her.

Then her eyes got huge. "**THEY ARE CHASING US!**" she screamed. I didn't dare look back.

"This way!" yelled Regina, running just behind Zoe. Her butterfly wings were flapping in the air behind her. I almost expected her to take flight. I wished that she could, and that she could take all of us with her. I was pretty sure zombies couldn't fly.

We ran back into the gem room. "In here!"

said Regina, leading us to a cupboard I hadn't noticed earlier. "Quick!"

"Can we all fit?" said Bernard.

"We'll find out! **COME ON!**" said Regina.

We all climbed in, squeezing close together, and then Regina tried to pull the door shut.

It wouldn't close.

"I'll hold it as closed as I can," she whispered. "But nobody move!"

"I don't like small spaces," Bernard moaned.

"You like them better than you'd like being zombie food!" said Ralph.

"You'll be okay," added Zoe. "Right, Sam?"

"Right," I said, even though I was pretty sure we were **DEFINITELY <u>NOT</u>** okay.

The cupboard was open a crack, just enough for us to see out.

"This way we can see them, but they can't see us," Regina said.

"Do you think the zombies can smell us in here?" whispered Zoe.

"I hope not," said Ralph.

"Everyone quiet!" I whispered as loud as I dared. "They're coming!"

Three zombies came in to the gem room, and paused, looking around. They looked almost human, if you ignored the fact that they also looked dead.

"One of them is coming closer!" said Zoe.

I couldn't see them very clearly through the crack in the cupboard and the dim light, but I could see them getting closer. I shut my eyes very tight.

"Everyone hold your breath," I whispered. "Just in case they can hear us breathing."

Everyone around me took a deep breath and then went very still.

After about ten seconds, I realized holding our breaths was a terrible idea. I already needed to breathe, and I was worried if I held my breath any longer I'd pass out and flop out of the cupboard.

I counted to ten again. I was starting to feel dizzy.

"They're gone!" Regina whispered suddenly, and we all exhaled.

"Are you sure?" I said.

"Let's wait another minute," said Zoe.

"I've got to get out of here, zombies or no zombies!" said Bernard, and he burst out of the cupboard and collapsed on the museum floor.

"Quick! Close the cupboard door!" said
Ralph. "Now we can call fit in here!"

I stuck my hand out to keep him from
closing the door. "That isn't how this crew
does things," I said sternly. "We'd never leave
Bernard out there on his own!"

"Thanks, Sam," said Bernard from the floor.

"We need to find a safe place," I said. "To make a plan."

"We don't need a plan," Ralph said. "We need to find the grown-ups. We need to get out of here!"

"We can't just leave," said Regina. "We have to go back to the party to warn the others!"

"That's why we need a plan," I said. "To figure out what we're doing first. This is what all our training has prepared us for."[12]

"What training?" scoffed Ralph. "All we did was go down my basement steps and run away! And even now our big grand plan is just to do research! All we have is a plan for a plan! We don't have **ANY** idea what we're doing!"

"We might be the earth's only hope!" I said. And then something occurred to me.

---

[12] This is something **Spaceman Jack** says on SPACE BLASTERS when him and **Captain Jane** are going into space battles.

"That's it! This is the zombie army from your basement! They must have got out! And it wasn't just zombie werewolves down there. It was regular zombies too!"

"You mean the zombie werewolf escaped?" said Regina.

I nodded solemnly. "I mean *everything* escaped."

"I didn't see the zombie werewolf with those zombies," said Zoe.

"We weren't in there long enough to do a full check," I said. "But I bet it's in there."

"I don't know Sam," said Bernard. "It could be **ANYWHERE**."

We all stared at each other as we realized what this meant. The zombie werewolf was on the loose **AND** there was a zombie army after us.

And it was up to us to save everyone.

CHAPTER 15

BREAK IN CASE OF EMERGENCY

"What are we going to do?" wailed Bernard.

Ralph jutted his chin towards me. "Ask our fearless Captain," he said. "He's the one who got us into this mess."

"You are the one who has zombie werewolves in your house! We wouldn't even be at this party if it wasn't for you," said Zoe, getting increasingly loud. She always gets loud when she gets nervous.

"Because we thought you could help us!" said Regina, looking a little upset.

"Everyone calm down," I said as firmly as I could, even though my hands were sweaty and shaking and I was pretty sure that there was no way we were going to get out of this alive. But I know from **SPACE BLASTERS** that a Captain **NEVER** shows their fear. They stay calm, cool and collected. Or at least that is what **Captain Jane** says. I took a deep breath and looked every member of my crew in the eyes, one by one. "We can't turn on each other," I said once everyone was quiet. "That is exactly what they want."

"What they want is to **EAT US**," said Zoe.

"That isn't helpful," said Bernard.

"Sorry," said Zoe. "Okay, Sam, what were you saying?"

They all stared at me and I suddenly felt

responsible for the **WHOLE WORLD**. "Well," I said, stalling a little bit, "does anyone have any ideas?"

"Guessing that means you don't have an idea," said Ralph. "I should have known."

"Now isn't the time to argue!" said Regina. "The zombies could come back in here at **ANY MINUTE**."

"Or they could have already made it to the party!" said Zoe. "We should go that way, and try to tell as many people as we can. And then we should get **OUT OF HERE**."

"Zoe is right," I said. "We have to save the others if we can."

"But what if we run into the zombies on our way back to the party?" said Bernard.

"Or what if they corner us?" said Regina.

"I can't believe we came so unprepared,"
I said. "If we had all our gear from the other
day, at least we'd have a chance. But we don't
have any silver. No Squirt Master XL. Not even
any flashlights!"

"Water!" said Ralph suddenly.

"Ralph, now is not the time to worry about
being thirsty," scolded Regina.

"No! **WATER!** Sam, you thought maybe
water could slow down the zombies or
something, right? And we want to get everyone
out of the building, right?" Ralph went on,
getting more excited as he spoke.

"Yes . . . " I said, unsure how these things
were connected.

"Then it's simple," said Ralph with a smug smile.
"WILL YOU JUST SPIT IT OUT?"

shouted Zoe. "**WE DON'T HAVE TIME FOR RIDDLES!**"

"It's really very obvious," Ralph said.

"Ralph," said Regina.

"We just need to pull the fire alarm and set off the sprinklers," said Ralph. "The water will melt the zombies and the alarm will get everyone out of the building."

"Commander Ralph," I said slowly, "that's **GENIUS!**"

"I know," said Ralph. But he was smiling.

Part of me was a tiny bit jealous that I hadn't thought of this, but most of me was just happy we had a plan.

A plan to save everyone!

"But . . . what about all the artefacts in the museum?" said Bernard, looking anxious. "Will they get ruined?"

"Bernard, if we don't stop the zombie apocalypse there won't be anyone to enjoy the museum!" said Zoe.

"Good point," said Bernard.

"And don't worry," said Regina, patting Bernard on the shoulder. "I know from my mum that the sprinklers here are special and won't damage anything."

"Can we stop discussing the sprinklers and just pull the alarm already?" said Ralph.

"Ralph is right," I said,[13] looking around the room. "Where is the nearest fire alarm?"

"There! In the corner!" said Zoe.

"Let's go over there together," said Regina. "Safety in numbers, remember?"

I glanced around the room to make sure

---

[13] A sentence I NEVER thought I would say.

there weren't any hiding zombies. "The coast is clear," I said. "Let's go!"

We all ran over to the fire alarm. It was big and red and behind glass. Next to the glass, hanging on the wall, was a tiny hammer.

"BREAK GLASS IN CASE OF EMERGENCY," read Bernard. "Well, this certainly is an emergency."

I looked at Ralph. "You can do it," I said. "Since it was your idea."

Ralph grabbed the hammer. "I've always wanted to break one of these," he said, as he smashed the

glass box.

Immediately, a high-pitched alarm went off.

"Is that it?" I said, looking around for the water.

"Almost," said Ralph, and then he pulled the red lever that had been behind the glass.

Another alarm went off, and sprinklers lowered from the ceiling.

We stared up at them for a second, and then with a **WHOOSH**, they began to spray water everywhere.

"We did it!" I shouted, high-fiving Ralph.

"Come on," said Regina, covering her head with her butterfly wings. "Let's get out of here and warn the others. This way!"

As we followed Regina down the corridor, all with our hands over our heads to try to keep off the water sprinkling from the ceiling,

I heard something. Muffled shouts, and what sounded like running.

A **LOT** of running.

I wanted to close my eyes and hide, but I forced myself to look over my shoulder.

And I saw the scariest thing **EVER**.

CHAPTER 16

MELTING ZOMBIES

Hundreds of zombies were running right toward us! **AGAIN!**

It was like a zombie stampede.

Our water plan had sort of worked. Some of them had melting faces, but they were still standing. Worse than standing. They were still running.

"*GO FASTER!*" I yelled at the top of my lungs. "**THE WATER DIDN'T STOP THEM! IT JUST MADE THEM MAD!**"

We burst out of the corridor into the

181

dinosaur exhibit we had been in earlier. Kids were running around yelling, the crisps were all getting wet, and the streamers and spider webs had all come down.

"Ralph! Regina! Where have you been?"

It was Mrs Zinkerman and she looked **MAD**. But I was so happy to see her! She could use her zombie hunter skills to save us! I ran up to her.

"Mrs Zinkerman! We need your help! An **ARMY OF ZOMBIES** is on the loose! They are right behind us, they'll be here any second."

Instead of springing into action like I thought she would, she just stared at me.

"It's okay!" I said, believing she still thought she had to hide her secret life from us. "We know all about the zombie werewolf you have trapped in your basement. And we know you and Mr Zinkerman are really zombie hunters."

She kept staring at me. "Sam," she said very slowly. "What on earth are you talking about?"

And then I heard the shouting of the zombie army behind us. "**THEY'RE HERE**!" I screamed. "**WE HAVE TO RUN!**"

"**MUM, WE HAVE TO GET OUT OF HERE!**" yelled Ralph, grabbing his mum's hand. "Where's Dad? Why are people still in here? We pulled the alarm so people would leave!"

"*Who* pulled the alarm?" said Mrs Zinkerman, still completely unconcerned about the fact that I'd just told her about the oncoming zombie army. She was also starting to sound more mad than I'd ever heard her.

"We did," I said quickly. "To save everyone! We thought that maybe the water would melt the zombies but I don't think it is working the way we thought it would. So now we have to get out of here! And you have to fight all the zombies!"

Mrs Zinkerman stared down at us. "You did *what?*" she said.

I started to explain again, but before I could, there was a commotion at the door.

And then the zombies burst in.

"**DO YOU SEE?**" I said, pointing at them.

"Darlings," said Mrs Zinkerman, still sounding not very happy at all. "Those are party guests. Not zombies." She rubbed her temples.

"Mum," said Ralph indignantly, "I know what a zombie looks like. Those are zombies."

"Can we stop arguing about if they are zombies or not and just get out of here?" said Regina, looking anxious.

"I'll prove it to you," said Mrs Zinkerman. Then she looked up and **WAVED AT ONE OF THE ZOMBIES**. "Charles! Charles, could you come over here?"

"Why is your mum friends with the zombies?" whispered Bernard. "**IS YOUR MUM A ZOMBIE?**"

Charles the Zombie came over. His face was green and melting and a piece of his head was missing, and he was wearing a tuxedo.

We all took a step back, but then Mrs Zinkerman took a step forward. She **HAD** to be a zombie hunter. How else could she stay so calm?

"Oh, you do look a fright! No wonder the children were afraid," she said, reaching **TOWARDS THE ZOMBIE** and grabbing

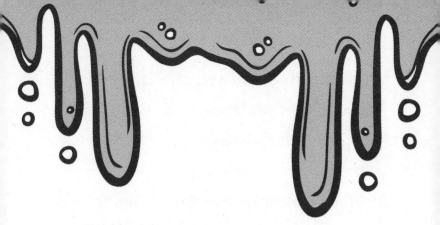

something out of his front pocket.

It was a handkerchief.

"What is your mum doing?" hissed Zoe.

Mrs Zinkerman took the handkerchief and raised it to Charles the Zombie's face, and with a sudden sinking feeling I knew exactly what she was going to do.

Mrs Zinkerman rubbed at Charles' face. The handkerchief came away green. And underneath – was human skin.

Now that I was looking at him up close, I could tell that he was, in fact, not a zombie, but a human dressed as a zombie.

Which, now that I thought about it, made a lot of sense on Halloween.

"Do you know what is going on?" said Charles the Not Zombie. "Sprinklers came on out of nowhere! Is there a fire?"

"I don't think there is a fire," Mrs Zinkerman said, in a very calm voice. But it is the kind of calm voice grown-ups use when they are actually very mad and trying to hide it. "Could you be a dear and please tell everyone else that there is no fire, and that the party will start up again shortly?"

Charles nodded and walked back towards the other zombies.

Who were also very clearly Not Zombies.

Mrs Zinkerman looked down at all of us. "I believe you all have some explaining to do," she said. "But before I can hear what I hope is a **VERY GOOD** explanation for what happened tonight, I need to help sort out things here. Go sit by the T-Rex. And *stay* there."

We sat in silence, none of us wanting to admit quite how wrong we had been. A couple of minutes later, the alarms suddenly stopped ringing and the sprinklers switched off. A voice came on over a loudspeaker.

"HALLOWEEN GALA GUESTS,
THE ALARM WAS PULLED BY ACCIDENT.
PLEASE MAKE YOUR WAY BACK TO THE PART
THE FLOORS ARE BEING MOPPED UP
AND FRESH FOOD AND DRINK
WILL BE PROVIDED SHORTLY."

Bernard spoke up first. "But what about the zombies in your basement?" he said quietly. "How do we explain those?"

"They must still be down there," said Regina, but she didn't sound very sure of herself.

"It is so obvious they were all in costumes!"

said Zoe. "How did we miss it?"

"It was dark in there," I said quickly. "It was a very easy mistake to make."

"We did the right thing," said Regina. "My parents will understand. They can't get mad at us for trying to save the whole world!"

"Exactly," I said. "And let's focus on the positive. At least we're all alive!"

We all had to high-five about that.

CHAPTER 17

UNDEAD AFTER ALL

As it turns out, you can get into quite a lot of trouble for trying to save the world.

After we explained everything that had happened to Mrs Zinkerman, complete with re-enactments of the most exciting parts, she pressed her lips together very tight and looked up at the ceiling.

"Darlings," she said, because Mrs Zinkerman is the kind of mum who says darlings even when she is very clearly not happy, "while I . . . applaud your creativity, I must admit,

193

I'm rather disappointed in your behaviour. You should have never have left the party in the first place. And, you *know* you should have never gone down to the basement without permission."

"But what **IS** in the basement?" I said, kind of hoping we could focus on that part and not the part about her being disappointed in us. Which I was pretty sure would lead to her telling our parents what had happened.

"I suppose the best thing to do is to show you," she said. "But," she went on, shaking her finger at us, "you are all in **VERY** big trouble. Especially you, Ralph Philip Zinkerman and Regina Georgina Zinkerman."

"We were just trying to help," Regina said in a very small voice.

Mrs Zinkerman sighed. "I know, darling. But you are still in trouble."

❧ ❧

We were *all* in trouble. Mrs Zinkerman called all of our parents to explain what had happened. And she also asked them to pick us up from Ralph and Regina's house instead of the museum. "Just so we can get this all sorted once and for all," she said as we climbed into her car.

❧ ❧

The Zinkermans' house looked even spookier at night. A full moon peeked out from behind the tallest turret.

Mr Zinkerman was already home, waiting for us in the kitchen. He had a stack of clothes in front of him.

"You probably all want to change out of your wet costumes," he said. "I've got some clean clothes for you here."

"You can't give away my clothes!" Ralph said indignantly.

"Ralph, you aren't in a position to be making demands," said Mr Zinkerman. "And do you really want your friends to be stuck in their wet things?"

"No," said Ralph sullenly. "But give them back," he added.

After we'd all changed and were dry, Mrs Zinkerman had hot chocolate ready in the kitchen. "This doesn't mean you aren't all in trouble," she said. "But, you've had quite the night, and I want to make sure you all get warm and can calm down a little bit too."

"How can we calm down when there is a zombie werewolf **RIGHT BELOW US?**" I said. I knew what I'd seen down there! I might have been wrong about the zombie army in the museum, but I wasn't wrong about this. I was sure about it.

"A what?" said Mr Zinkerman, looking very confused.

"It's a long story," said Mrs Zinkerman. "I'll let the kids tell you about it later, but for now, we need to take them down to the basement. I don't think anyone is going to calm down until we do."

"Does the suit of armour have anything to do with this?" said Mr Zinkerman.

197

"We were taking precautions!" I said. "We probably should do the same thing tonight. We can't go into the basement unprepared!"

"We'll be fine. I promise," said Mrs Zinkerman. "Now, follow me."

∽ ∾

The first surprise in the basement was when Mrs Zinkerman flipped on a light at the top of the stairs.

"Guess we didn't need that flashlight," said Bernard.

"How could we have known there was a light switch there?" I said.

The next surprise was all the animals.

Staring up at us with beady eyes were three bears, five foxes, and one very large wolf.

"We've been storing some of the taxidermy

animals for the museum," said Mr Zinkerman. "I've been restoring them. It's one of my hobbies."

"That's a weird hobby," said Bernard, staring at the wolf. "But my dad likes to clean old rocks, so I guess grown-ups like weird things."

"Are those . . . dead?" said Zoe.

"Technically, yes," said Mr Zinkerman. "They are specimens from the museum. They've been dead a long time though. And then they are stuffed and preserved."

"So they *are* undead!" I exclaimed. "They have been basically zombies!"

"No, Sam," said Mr Zinkerman, but he was smiling. "They are more like the stuffed animal toys you have at home."

"I don't have anything like this at home,"
I said.

"I'll never be able to look at my
teddy the same way," said Zoe,
eyeing one of the bears.

Just then, the whistling, grumbling, howling sound that we'd heard the last time we'd been in the basement started up.

Ralph and Regina's parents stayed calm, but the rest of us all jumped.

"That's the noise!" said Regina. "The zombie werewolf! It must be in here somewhere! It's hiding!"

"That, my dear, is our boiler," said Mr Zinkerman. He pointed at a huge boiler in the corner, which was shaking and creaking and . . . howling. "We probably need to get it repaired, it's been making a terrible racket for weeks."

"The **BOILER?**" I said. I couldn't believe we thought that the boiler was a zombie werewolf!

"I'm afraid so, Sam," said Mr Zinkerman. "Sorry to disappoint you. I know a zombie werewolf would have been much more exciting."

"And I'm sorry that we aren't zombie hunters," said Mrs Zinkerman. "I quite like the sound of that."

"But . . . but . . . why aren't we allowed down here then?" said Ralph.

Mr and Mrs Zinkerman exchanged a look.

"If we tell you," said Mr Zinkerman, "you have to promise you won't try to sneak down here."

Ralph and Regina nodded.

"This is where we hide your birthday presents! We can't keep them lying around where you might see them."

Ralph immediately started looking around the room. "My birthday present is down here?"

"Ralph! This is why we have to hide them. We don't want to ruin the surprise," said Mrs Zinkerman.

"And, there are a lot of chemicals and tools involved in taxidermy. It's not exactly safe for you to be running around down here. Although, I should have known that as soon as we told you it was off limits, you'd want to come in," added Mr Zinkerman.

I scratched my head. My thoughts were whirling and I was trying to make sense of everything. "So . . . the sound we heard was the boiler," I said. "And the shapes we saw were these . . . undead giant stuffed animals that belong in the museum. And the zombies at the party . . . "

"The theme of the party for the adults was actually The Undead. Quite fitting, if you think about it," said Mrs Zinkerman.

"And the hole in the door?" Regina asked.

Mr Zinkerman laughed. "That is my fault, I'm afraid. I was bringing up a spear that I'd repaired from one of the exhibitions, and wasn't paying attention. It went straight through the door!"

"Wow," I said, because I didn't know what else to say.

Then the doorbell rang.

"That will be one of your parents," said Mrs Zinkerman. "Let's go back up to the kitchen so you can finish your hot chocolate, and we can discuss with your parents an appropriate punishment."

~ ⁓

In the end, all our parents decided it was only fair if we all had the same punishment. And that punishment was to write apology notes to EVERY guest who had been at the party, and to come back to the Zinkermans' house every Saturday for the next month and rake the leaves in their giant back garden. There were so many leaves I was pretty sure we'd be raking leaves for the rest of our lives. And even though we were supposed to all have the same punishment, my mum also said I couldn't watch **SPACE BLASTERS** for two whole weeks!

I didn't regret what we'd done though. Like **Spaceman Jack** would say, sometimes being a hero isn't always appreciated. And you can't do it for the glory. You have to do it because it is the right thing to do. Sure, this time we might have been wrong, but it was worth it.

The next day we went over to Ralph and Regina's house like we all said we would. Their parents handed us all rakes and we went out into the back garden.

"Is this a graveyard?" said Zoe, staring at what looked a lot like a tombstone.

"Yep!" said Regina cheerfully. "Everyone in our family is buried out here."

"Oh," said Zoe, her eyes wide. "Um. Cool."

"You're standing on Great-Aunt Gertrude," said Regina, pointing. Zoe hopped off the stone she was standing on.

"We should probably get started," said

Bernard, looking around us.

There were at least a **MILLION** leaves. They were all different colours too. Red and orange and yellow. They crunched under our feet.

Raking leaves wasn't too bad. It was actually kind of fun. Especially because whenever we made a pile of leaves that was big enough, we'd jump in it.

It was nice to know that no matter what I did with my friends, I could have fun.

"Hey Sam Wu," said Ralph, and as I turned he threw a bunch of leaves at me. But not in a really mean way. In an almost-friend way. I laughed, and threw leaves back. I noticed that he hadn't even said Sam Wu-ser.

It was funny, being almost-sort-of friends

with Ralph.

We jumped and played in the leaves and kind of raked all afternoon. I decided coming over here every Saturday might not be that bad.

"Hey Sam," said Regina, as she jumped into a big pile of leaves we'd just raked.

"What?" I said as I jumped in next to her.

"I bet there really is a zombie werewolf out

there somewhere," she said. "And I bet we could face it."

"Definitely," I said.

Because I'm Sam Wu, and I am **NOT** afraid.

ACKNOWLEDGEMENTS

We love writing Sam Wu – but we couldn't have made it into a real book that you can hold in your hands without the help and support of some amazing people!

If we had our own spaceship on **SPACE BLASTERS**, our captain would be Claire Wilson, our fearless agent who always guides us in the right direction. Thank you for believing in us and believing in Sam Wu.

We are tremendously grateful to everyone at our publisher Egmont for supporting Sam Wu. Thank you to our brilliant editors Lindsey Heaven and Ali Dougal.

Huge thank you to our incredibly talented illustrator Nathan Reed for bringing Sam and his friends to life on the page! The illustrations are our favourite part of the book and they somehow keep getting better and better! We are very lucky authors. We especially love all the zombies and the dinosaur skeletons in this book. Nathan, you are the best!

Thank you as well to our wonderful designer, Margaret Hope, who made the pages look so awesome. And special thanks to Lucy Courtenay for her eagle-eyed copyedits. Big thank you to the publicity, sales and marketing teams for their support, especially Hilary Bell and Olivia Carson.

We'd like to thank our families and friends for all their support and excitement.

And to our daughter, Evie, to whom this book is dedicated. We love you.